Meet Monster

Six Stories about the
World's Friendliest Monster

by **Ellen Blance** and **Ann Cook**
illustrated by **Quentin Blake**

Marshall Cavendish Children

For Chelsea and Felicity   —E. B.

For Jessica, Beka & Abigail   —A. C.

The authors believe that initial reading experiences should be closely linked to the spoken language of children. Therefore, the Monster stories draw upon the words and expressions used by children from five to eight years old as they talked with the authors about Monster and his adventures.

First published in 1973 in the United States by Bowmar Publishing Corporation
First Marshall Cavendish Classics edition, 2011

Marshall Cavendish Corporation, 99 White Plains Road, Tarrytown, NY 10591

Marshall Cavendish *Classics*

Marshall Cavendish is bringing classic titles from children's literature back into print for a new generation. We have selected titles that have withstood the test of time, and we welcome any suggestions for future titles in this program. To learn more, visit our Web site: www.marshallcavendish.us/kids

Library of Congress Cataloging-in-Publication Data
Blance, Ellen.
Meet monster : six stories about the world's friendliest monster / by Ellen Blance and Ann Cook; illustrated by Quentin Blake. — 1st Marshall Cavendish classics ed. v. cm.
Summary: Monster decides to move to a new city, and soon he has found a house to live in and makes new friends.
Contents: Monster comes to the city — Monster looks for a house — Monster cleans his house — Monster looks for a friend — Monster meets Lady Monster — Monster and the magic umbrella.
ISBN 978-0-7614-5648-3
[1. Moving, Household—Fiction. 2. Monsters—Fiction. 3. Friendship—Fiction. 4. City and town life—Fiction.] I. Cook, Ann, 1940– II. Blake, Quentin, ill. III. Title.
PZ7.B589Mee 2011
[E]—dc22
2010014799

Book design by Vera Soki
Editor: Marilyn Brigham

Printed in Malaysia (T)
1 3 5 6 4 2

Marshall Cavendish
Children

contents

BOOK #1

Monster comes to the City

Once upon a time there was a city.

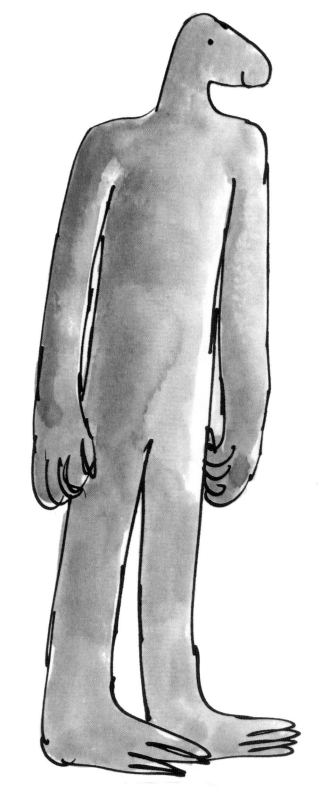

A monster comes to this city
to live.

Monster is not ugly
like other monsters.
He's very tall,
and his head is skinny.

Monster goes around the city to
see the river and the houses
and everything.

10

He goes up the lamp post to see the houses and the cars.

He goes to the railway station
to see the trains and everything.

He goes to see
what the people look like.

Then he goes to the park
to play with the kids
swinging on the swings.

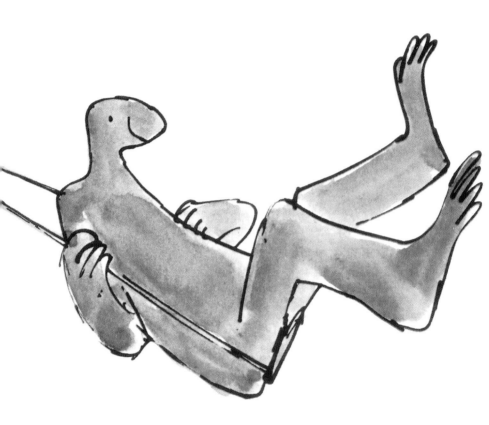

He looks at all the shops and
clothes and things.

He packs all his things.

Monster thinks the city is fine.
He thinks he will live here.

BOOK #2

MONSTER LOOKS FOR A HOUSE

Once upon a time there was a city.
A monster comes to live in this city.

He looks at the map.
He wants to find a place to live.

He is going on the bus to see
where he wants to live.

He thinks he likes this street.
He might be able to live here.

He looks at all the houses.

This house is dark all over.
Not many things happen in
this house.

He can't live here.

29

He likes the bell on the top of this house, but this house is too big for him.

He can't live here.

This house is a mess.

Monster can't live here.

Monster finds a pretty house
that is too little for him.
It is too little.
He could hardly fit in here.

Monster can't live here.

He might be able to live in
this house.

It's tall and thin.
The windows and the door are
just right for him.

He goes into the house.
He says it's okay for him.
It's very comfortable.
It's very, very fine.
So he will live in it.

BOOK #3

MONSTER CLEANS HIS HOUSE

Monster lives in a tall, thin
house in the city.
He loves the house.
It's very, very fine.

He's got a bedroom,
a bathroom, a closet,
a living room, and a kitchen.

It's very nice for a monster.
It's very comfortable.
Monster loves the house.

He's reading a book about monsters.

He should read a monster book,
because he's a monster himself.

46

He thinks he will clean the house
so that if children want to visit him,
it will look really fine.

He cleans the bedroom so that
if people come to stay, he won't
have to clean the bedroom when
they are sleeping.

He cleans the kitchen so that
when people come over and
want to cook for Monster, they can.
The kitchen won't be a mess.

He cleans the bath so that when people come in to have a bath, they won't get dirty. When they pour the water in, the water will be clean.

He cleans out the closet so that people can put their clothes inside, and the clothes won't get dirty.

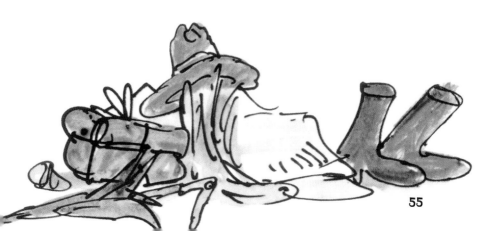

Monster thinks he's done enough cleaning. He's very tired and sits down.

The house looks really fine.

BOOK #4

MONSTER LOOKS for a FRIEND

Monster loves his house.
He likes to eat his breakfast
in bed.

He is thinking about what he should do today.

Monster thinks he will go out to play soccer.

Monster plays soccer for
a long time.

He loves playing soccer,
but it is no fun by himself.

He sits on the ball,
and he is
very, very sad.

He goes out of the house to
find somebody to play with.
He takes his umbrella and goes
out to look for a friend.
He goes down all the streets to
see if there are any kids to
play with, but there aren't any.

Monster doesn't know why.

He looks in the houses, but he
can't find anybody to play with.

He looks in the park, but he can't find anybody to play with.

Monster comes back to his house.

He is sad.
He is really, really sad, because he
can't find anybody to play with.

But at the door of his house is this little boy.

"Maybe he wants to play," says Monster.

The little boy says that he likes the house.
He says to Monster, "Can I live in it?"

So Monster says, "Sure.
Sure, you can live with me.
You're my best friend."

And they shake hands.

BOOK #5

MONSTER MEETS LADY MONSTER

Monster says he wants to
clean up the house.

The little boy wants to go
play outside.
He wants to play soccer
instead of cleaning up the house.

He think it's no fun
cleaning up the house.

Monster gives the little boy
an apron. Monster says,
"Here, put on your apron so
you can help me. You can
clean the windows."

The little boy looks angry.
Maybe he is sad.

The little boy looks out of the window.

He sees another monster, a lady monster.

He didn't know there was such a thing as a lady monster.

The lady monster is jumping rope
with two hands,
and her feet are going
up and down.

She is pretty.

The little boy goes upstairs to
tell Monster.

But Monster can't hear him.

So the little boy yells,
"There's a lady monster
outside!"

But Monster still can't hear him.
So he yells in Monster's ear,

"There's a lady monster outside!"

"There's a lady monster outside!"

"There's
a
lady
monster
outside!"

Monster is happy.
He is so, so happy.

He goes into the bathroom
and brushes his teeth
and brushes his hair
and puts on his beautiful tie.

He goes outside.
Then he says,
"Can I be your friend?"

The lady monster says,
"I'd be glad to be your friend."

Then Monster falls in
love with the lady monster.
And they jump rope together
and have a very nice time.

BOOK #6

MONSTER and the MAGIC umbrella

One day Monster and the little
boy get out of bed.

The day is so hot.
The sun is shining.
Monster says, "Come on,
let's wash and get dressed so
we can go outside and play."

So that's what they do.

It is such a hot day.
Monster takes his best hat
and his umbrella to keep the
sun off his face.

Then everyone plays soccer.
The sun is shining on them.
They smell sweaty.

Their mothers call them for
dinner, and all the boys and
all the girls go home.

Monster and the little boy
feel so hot.

The little boy says, "Oh,
Monster, I feel so hot."

So Monster opens the umbrella
to keep the sun off their faces.
"Now it'll be much cooler,"
Monster says.

So that's what Monster does.
He just opens his umbrella.

The umbrella starts to grow
bigger . . .

. . . and bigger.
Then Monster turns it around.

Boy, isn't it giant-sized?

Super big!

The little boy and Monster
just look at the umbrella.

Then the little boy says,
"Oh, Monster, I wish we had a
swimming pool to swim in. I'm
so hot."

Suddenly it starts raining.
Big drops of water
fall in the umbrella.

The little boy says,
"Oh, wow, doesn't that look like
a swimming pool?
Let's take off our socks and
shoes and jump in and swim."

Monster says, "Yes, why not?"

The water is cool.
It feels so good.

The boys and girls come back
out. All the boys and all the girls
take their shoes off.
They jump in and splash in
the water up and down.
Up and down.

Then everybody says,
"Home for bed, home for bed.
Let's do this tomorrow.
This was really fun."

So the umbrella gets smaller
and smaller . . .

and tinier . . .

and tinier.

The umbrella isn't a
magic umbrella anymore.

Then Monster and the little boy
go home.

The End

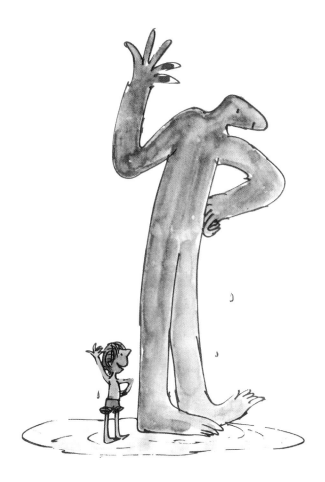